ETHAN TUCKER'S JOB

Also by Kevin Matthew Hayes

Mystery/Modern Western
Live Oak Key

All Hallows' Eve Tales
The Beast of Talbotton
Reckonings
Facing Demons

Poetry
Summer 2020
July 4, 2020
Day Dreaming
The Forts of Pensacola Bay
Nightfall at Pensacola Beach
Blackwater River State Park
Are You Prepared for All Hallows' Eve?
The Legend of Ole Stingy Jack

Ethan Tucker's Job

KEVIN MATTHEW HAYES

ISBN: 978-1-965315-09-5 (paperback)
ISBN: 978-1-965315-10-1 (hardcover)
ISBN: 978-1-965315-15-6 (e-book)

This is a work of fiction. Names, characters, businesses, places, events, locales, and incidents are either the products of the author's imagination or used fictitiously. Any resemblance to actual persons, living or dead, or actual events is purely coincidental.

Published by:
Live Oak Key Publishing LLC / LiveOakKeyPublishingLLC.com

Proofread by:
Proofed.com

Book cover design and layout by:
Ellie Bockert Augsburger / CreativeDigitalStudios.com

Cover design features stock images by:
Daria / stock.adobe.com
subinpumsom / stock.adobe.com
Elena / stock.adobe.com
Elscar Studios / stock.adobe.com

Author portrait by:
Matt Keene / St. Augustine Tintype

Published by Live Oak Key Publishing LLC

www.liveoakkeypublishingllc.com

Live Oak Key Publishing LLC was established in July 2024 by author Kevin Matthew Hayes. His passion is to publish stories based on the history, legends, and culture of the American South and American West.

Visit our website to shop other titles and merchandise, and follow our socials.

"Have you considered my servant Job, that there is none like him on the earth, a blameless and upright man, who fears God and turns away from evil."

Job 1:8

PROLOGUE

A light breeze with a hint smell of the sea made the hot and humid night in St. Marks somewhat more bearable. The streets were almost empty in the small coastal town except for a few people working late or looking for a good time. At the docks, a ranch foreman began talking with the sheriff.

The foreman held a lantern up to one of the cattle's brands. "Do you see this, sheriff? This brand has been changed. I know because I worked for this ranch down around Pine Level."

"When were these cattle delivered?" asked the sheriff. He was an older gentleman who dressed more like a politician. He sported a three-piece suit with a black tie. Many would not think much of the aged sheriff by judging his peaceful-looking face, but others knew he had a reputation for a quick draw that could put down out-of-hand sailors who were looking to get into trouble.

"They came off that steamer this afternoon," replied the foreman. He pointed toward a small steamboat anchored in the harbor. The foreman was a rough-looking man. His clothes, wool hat, and knee-high boots looked new given he had moved to the area recently, but his face showed scares reminiscent of the rough south Florida frontier from which he came. "There were four of them. The man in charge was named Alaster Conley. He is the one that completed the sale."

"Did any of the sailors say anything about these men?" asked the sheriff.

"No, you know how they are when they arrive. When they get paid, they head right for town."

"Did you see where they went?"

"After my boss had paid Alaster for the cattle, Alaster turned around and paid his men. His men talked about visiting the bordello with the sailors. Alaster mentioned something about playing cards at the saloon."

"Let me go talk with Mr. Conley and see if we can get this figured out."

"Be careful, sheriff. I know the type. These are some rough cowboys. Sometimes they don't take kindly to the law."

***

The moon was full and at its peak in the sky. The rumbles from a distant storm over the Gulf could be heard in the distance. The clock struck midnight as the sheriff entered the saloon. The double-action door swung shut behind the sheriff as the sounds of his boots stepping on the wooden floor echoed throughout the room. The bartender was busy drying dishes, and there were two cardplayers sitting at a table in the far corner. The well-dressed cardplayer sitting with his back to the wall was well-known in town and a regular at the saloon. Looking much like a wealthy plantation owner, he was a professional cardplayer and gambled on riverboats throughout the region. He had managed to make his own fortune but never worried about money, considering the wealth his family had accumulated.

The other man with his back toward the entrance was Alaster Conley. His wide-brimmed wool hat was full of dirt and grease and hanging on the chair next to him. His hickory shirt and cotton pants were torn in some spots, and his boots extended above his knees. His spurs were a showy Spanish style and possibly stolen. They were too fancy for this cowboy.

The sheriff looked directly at the back of the cowboy. He paused for a moment and placed his hand on his revolver but kept it in his holster.

"Mr. Conley," called the sheriff.

Alaster froze for a moment. He appeared to be staring directly at the cardplayer. The smoke from his lit cigarette rose at a slight angle above his head and danced above him due to the thick, humid air.

"Mr. Conley," said the sheriff. "I need to ask you a couple of questions about the cattle you sold earlier today."

Alaster still refused to move. He just sat in the same position like a stone. The cardplayer opposite Alaster sat still as well. He looked right into Alaster's face. He knew the type and had gambled with them before. He figured Alaster was wanted somewhere. He never discriminated against anyone concerning their background as long as they were willing to play a good hand of cards, a rule he was beginning to regret on this night. He could tell Alaster was ready to draw blood.

The cardplayer glanced quickly at the sheriff. The sheriff read his eyes. Alaster was going to draw. Alaster lifted a revolver out of his lap, turned, aimed, and fired from under his left shoulder. The old sheriff had his Colt out of its holster and was ready to fire at Alaster when the bullet struck him in the heart. He hit the ground dead. Blood began to flow across the floor from the exit wound.

Alaster turned back toward the cardplayer and was greeted with the barrel of a pocket pistol. The cardplayer fired, and the ball just grazed Alaster's cheek. Alaster, angered at the cheap shot, aimed his revolver at the cardplayer and fired twice. The bullets thrust the cardplayer back to the wall with his arms extended out like a sign of forgiveness. Blood splattered on the wall behind him, and his body bent forward in the chair and came to a rest on the tabletop.

Alaster looked at the bartender behind the counter. He was in shock at the sight and stepped backward until his back was against the wall. The scene that seemed to play out in slow motion only lasted several seconds.

Alaster looked back at the table, stood up, put his cigarette out, and downed his shot of whiskey. Then he placed his revolver back in his belt, picked up all the money at the table, packed it together neatly, folded it, and put it in his pocket. Then he proceeded to rob the cardplayer of his valuables and weapons.

Alaster walked over to the sheriff and began to remove his Colt and belt when another man from outside yelled. Alaster froze in the middle of removing the belt. "This is the deputy. Both exits have gunmen on them. There is no place for you to go. If you throw up your hands and come out, we won't shoot you."

Alaster put the sheriff's belt over his left shoulder and held the other end with his left hand. He pointed the Colt at the bartender with his right hand. The bartender's eyes got big.

"Is there any way to get to the roof?" asked Alaster.

"There's a skylight in the hall upstairs."

Alaster grabbed his hat and headed up the stairs, with each step screeching from the loose boards. Once in the hall, he spotted the skylight. It looked like it came off an old ship, probably one that was decommissioned in the harbor.

He looked down both sides of the hall. The doors were all closed, and he figured if anyone was in the rooms; they were too afraid to come out. Alaster took a chair in the hall and placed it directly under the skylight. Then he used the butt of the sheriff's gun to bust the glass and frame. He tilted his hat above his eyes and blocked his face with his hand to protect himself from falling glass. Ship skylights often had brass bars extended over the glass to protect the windows from being busted at sea; fortunately for Alaster, the bars had long since been removed.

After the glass and window frames were busted out, Alaster grabbed the edge of the window sill, pulled himself up through the opening, and rolled his body onto the roof. His newly acquired gear made the roll appear somewhat awkward.

Alaster stood up and examined his surroundings. It was hard to make out in the lantern-lit street, but there appeared to be one man in front holding a revolver, the deputy, and another man at the back door. The man in the back had a long gun of some sort. The blacksmith's shop was right next door to the saloon. Despite the weight of his gear, Alaster felt he could make the jump and land on the roof of the blacksmith's shop.

Alaster quickly walked to the other end of the saloon to get a running start. He took a deep breath, prepped his mind for the jump, and started running. When he got to the edge of the building, he put both his feet on the ledge and leaped. He looked two stories down briefly before the next roof appeared beneath his feet. Alaster braced for the impact, hit the roof, and began to slide down the angled side. He pressed his boots against the shingles of the shop as if he were attempting to dig his boots into mud or sand. His descent on the roof slowed before he came to a stop.

He looked around and saw a dormer window above him. Alaster worked his way back up the roof toward the window, careful not to let his feet or hands slip out from under him or make any noise. When he got to the window, he was relieved to find that it was cracked open to let the heat out of the building. Alaster opened the window and entered.

The room was engulfed in darkness, and it was impossible to make anything out. He could hear the deputy and some other men talking outside. A crowd was beginning to fill the street in front of the saloon. Alaster fumbled in the darkness and reached into his pocket to pull out a match. When Alaster lit it, he was greeted with an unpleasant sight.

The blacksmith was standing in the room holding a loaded double-barrel shotgun in Alaster's face—both barrels cocked and ready to fire. The blacksmith was a large and rough-looking man with dark hair and a thick dark beard. His clothes were stained and burned from his occupation, and he was wearing a leather apron and working late into the night.

The blacksmith yelled out to the deputy. "Deputy! I've got your man! He's upstairs in my shop!"

The blacksmith never took his eyes off Alaster. Alaster stood there with his arms halfway up in the air as a somewhat sign of surrender. He was frozen like earlier, with a match still burning in his hand, contemplating how he could get out of this situation.

The sounds of men running up the stairs resonated throughout the room before the door swung open. The deputy, a middle-aged man wearing shooter boots, cotton pants, and a button-down shirt with suspenders, entered. He looked as if he hurried over to assist the sheriff due to his lack of a hat and jacket. Another man followed with a long gun. He wasn't a deputy but was probably there to help out. He looked like a longshoreman judging from his attire.

Still excited about the entire incident, they both ran past the blacksmith while acknowledging him—his eyes still darting out toward Alaster. The longshoreman placed the barrel of his gun in Alaster's face, and the deputy fumbled to put his revolver away in his holster. Then he pulled out some handcuffs. He was still shaking from the events that had transpired. The deputy grabbed Alaster's arms, pulled them down, placed the handcuffs over his wrists, and locked the cuffs. Then he proceeded to remove Alaster's weapons. The deputy and the longshoreman led Alaster out of the room. They thanked the blacksmith for his help as they exited the building.

St. Marks was a quiet coastal town that rarely had incidents such as the one that unfolded tonight. Whether it was out of boredom, excitement, or just being plain nosey, everyone lined the streets so they could witness the episode firsthand and see the man responsible.

As Alaster was led down the street toward the jail, the deputy began to talk. "Do you have any idea who you shot?"

"A sheriff that made an unwise decision?" responded Alaster.

"I'm not talking about him," replied the deputy. "I'm talking about the man you were playing cards with."

"What about him?" responded Alaster.

"He's the son of a politician in Tallahassee. That man is going to want your head in a noose."

Just before they entered the jail, Alaster saw a familiar face. It was one of his men. He winked his eye once toward Alaster as a sign of assurance. Alaster knew it wouldn't be long before he was out.

Alaster was led into the building and toward his jail cell. At the entrance, the longshoreman held his gun at Alaster's face as the deputy removed the cuffs. He was then led into the cell, and the door was shut. One turn of the key by the deputy and a click signaled that Alaster was secure.

"As soon as morning arrives," started the deputy, "I'll get the judge so he can get started."

The deputy spoke to the longshoreman. "Stay here and keep an eye on him. If anyone enters and tries to cause trouble, fire a shot, and I'll be right back. I'm going to take care of the sheriff."

The deputy exited the building, and the longshoreman pulled a chair out from behind the desk and placed it in front of Alaster's cell. He sat down and put his gun in his lap. He refused to take his eyes off the criminal. He wanted to make sure nothing got past him and that justice would be served.

~ 1 ~

As I walked up the stairs outside the adjutant general's office, I took note of the gloomy weather and light rain and then lowered my hat just above my eyes—fine weather as if it were a lazy Sunday morning. The gloomy weather was moving northward from the Gulf. Under the roof of the porch, I stopped and took note of my surroundings—a wet day in Tallahassee. People were running their errands along the boardwalk in the weather. Horses and buggies ran up and down the street. The streets were full of mud and horse manure. I looked over at my poor horse at the hitching post. Its legs were covered in mud.

I turned and entered the office. I removed my hat and hung it on the coat rack. A young man about 18 in a suit was working at the desk.

"Mr. Tucker?" he asked.

"That's right," I replied.

"Let me tell the adjutant general you have arrived," he replied.

I heard the young secretary walk down the hall and knock on the adjutant general's door. His secretary cracked the door so as not to disturb him in case he was in the middle of something. He was trying to keep everything orderly, perhaps to impress his boss.

"Sir," began the secretary. "Mr. Tucker is here."

"Good," replied the adjutant general. "Send him in."

He shut the door and walked back to the entrance. "The adjutant general is ready for you. Please follow me."

I followed the secretary to the room, and he opened the door for me. After I entered, I heard the door close quietly and footsteps on the other side walking back down the hall. Adjutant General Ryder sat at his desk as the platter of rain on the rooftop echoed throughout the dark room.

I saw myself briefly in a mirror hanging on the wall. Despite my coming from a prominent family, I didn't look the part. I was dressed in a dark, relaxed cut, three-piece suit with paisley cravat hinting at my upbringing, but my hair was longer, my face was unshaven, and my knee-high boots were covered in mud. I had been working for the Tallahassee Railroad Company after I returned from the Third Seminole War. It required me to work in the office and on the line when there was an issue. A foreman, some would say.

"Still fighting with the wife, I see," replied Ryder.

Ryder stood up, and we shook hands. Then he waved toward a chair, signaling for me to sit. I sat down, he sat down in his chair behind his desk, and we continued to talk.

"She still won't let me in the house," I replied. "I've been living in the back of the roundhouse."

"Good Lord," replied Ryder. "How do you do that?"

"It's not bad. I have a cot and a chest full of my clothes."

"Isn't it noisy?"

"They haven't been running the trains at night. If they did, I don't think it would bother me. I would sleep right through the noise. Between helping manage the Tallahassee Railroad and keeping my farm together, I'm worn out."

"Have you two talked since you got back? It's been a few months since the war ended."

"Briefly. I stayed there for a couple of nights before she made me leave. She says south Florida and the last two wars with the Seminoles made me wild. She says she doesn't want me near the kids until I change my ways."

"Do you still read scripture at night?"

"Yes. I'm hoping it will help me improve. I've heard people say it will. To be honest, I have a hard time understanding it."

We both paused for a moment.

"You're probably wondering why I asked you here," began the adjutant general. "I've been in talks with Governor Perry. He wants to reorganize the state militia. You've probably heard the rumors about secession."

"I have," I replied. "Just when you wrap one up, they are ready to start another war. Those plantation owners are worried."

"I know," Ryder replied. "But we have a number of those people here in Tallahassee, and we need to be prepared just in case they can't settle their differences in Washington." The adjutant general paused for a second. He looked down at his desk and leaned back in his chair with his fingers clasped on his stomach. He looked back up, unsure of the response. "I want to give you another command." The clock in his office struck noon.

I hesitated to answer.

"I know you are having trouble at home," Ryder began. "But you are a good officer. You're seasoned from the last two Seminole Wars and the war with Mexico. Also, I can trust you. It's almost impossible to find people I can trust in this town. Everyone has their own agenda."

"Ryder, this is partly why my wife is mad at me. She says I was never home before."

"Ethan, I really need someone I can trust and who will get the job done."

I still remained hesitant.

"I can resort to conscription, if need be," said Ryder.

"What?" I replied. I looked right at him. I'm sure I had a puzzled look on my face.

"I'm sorry, Ethan, but I need you. I'm in a tight spot."

"You son of a bitch!"

"Sorry, Ethan, but the political world doesn't stop, and I don't have a choice."

"If I refuse?"

"By law, I can have you arrested. Might as well get ready for the draft. It's coming."

"Being a politician comes natural to you! What happened? I remember growing up with you. We were good friends."

"The capitol has that effect on people if you're here long enough."

I looked around the room. I thought about any other options I may have. Once I realized my situation was hopeless, I threw up my arms in surrender and put them back on the arms of my chair.

"What do you want me to do?"

"We had an incident take place in St. Marks last night. A cowboy gunned down the sheriff and a cardplayer. I need you to bring him back to Tallahassee so he can stand trial."

"That's an unusual request for the militia, don't you think?"

"Normally, yes, but the cardplayer happens to be the son of a representative here in Tallahassee, and he wants to ensure justice is carried out."

There was a brief pause.

"You politicians seem to enjoy your power."

"I know. The governor has been driving me up the wall since this morning. He wants me to do something for the representative's son."

"All of this because a politician's son can't stay out of trouble."

"That, and the governor needs his vote for some upcoming legislation."

"Right! Of course! You people are unbelievable."

Ryder leaned back in his chair again. "It's a swamp," he began. "And Perry is the biggest gator for now."

The adjutant general leaned forward, reached into the desk, and pulled out an envelope. He slid the envelope across the desk toward me, and I picked it up.

"Here are your orders. I've got some cash for expenses. Just show them my signature at the train station and they will give you passage to St. Marks. I want you to activate one of your former soldiers to help. The deputy down there has the cowboy locked up in jail. He is waiting for your arrival so he can transfer the prisoner to you."

"And after that?"

"Hand the prisoner over to the sheriff here in town. He will take care of him from that point. You and your soldier will be paid upon your return."

I stood up. "I'll get the job done, but our friendship is over."

"If that's how it has to be. For what it's worth, I'm sorry."

I turned and marched out of his office, slamming the door shut behind me.

$$\sim 2 \sim$$

I stopped in front of the gate and strapped my horse to the fence. A short wood picket fence surrounded the house, separating it from the fields that I tended to each day. I looked at my home in the damp weather. Memories of my past came to mind. I could see myself playing with my kids in the front yard under the large oak tree, with Spanish moss waving in the slight breeze on a late evening around dusk. The relief from the sun made for a relaxed time for all.

That's a distant memory now. I gained the courage I needed and opened the gate. A familiar squeak in the hinge signaled to my wife that someone had entered our yard. I walked down the brick walkway and up the stairs to our porch and knocked at the front door.

My wife, Faith, opened the door slightly. It was good to see her face again. Some people would say that she had aged some since the time we had met. To me, she still looked like the day I met her. Her fair skin was bright. Her blonde hair and blue eyes lifted my spirit briefly. She was wearing a blue dress with an apron that had a couple of stains. Between keeping house and raising our two boys, she looked tired. Her hair had been fixed at one point during the day but was beginning to fall as she prepared for the boys to arrive back from school.

She looked right at me through the cracked door. "No, Ethan, I don't have time for this today."

"Faith," I began. "I just need a couple of things."

Faith shut the door.

"Ethan," she replied. "The last time you were here, we argued for an hour. I don't need this."

"Faith," I began. "I just need my stuff from the trunk upstairs."

It got quiet on the other side of the door. Then the door swung open.

"You went back to the militia!"

"It's not like that, Faith. You don't understand."

"Your own family is upside down. I've thrown you out, and instead of seeking to make amends, you go right back to the militia with your friends."

"You don't understand, Faith. I don't have a choice."

"You haven't learned one thing! You haven't changed!"

She walked into the adjacent room next to the staircase and continued to talk.

"Go upstairs and get your stuff! The sooner you head back to south Florida, the better. Just get out before the boys get back from school."

I entered the house, walked upstairs to our bedroom, and thought about how to respond. I knew it wouldn't do any good. "I'm not even going to south Florida, just St. Marks."

When I entered the doorway of my old room, I looked around. The bed was neatly made, and everything was dust-free. I could tell she was working hard to raise the boys properly. She was trying to set an example. My trunk was at the end of the bed. I bent down and opened it. I could still hear Faith. She was no doubt cursing me lower than a dog. It sounded like she was digging through a closet.

The contents of the trunk were neatly put away as to pre-serve the items like a family scrapbook. My wool hat was on top, and my militia jacket and belt buckle were underneath. I remember when my wife sewed my jacket before I went to war. When I was given the commission of an officer in the state militia, the state only gave me a box of gold gilt buttons and a belt buckle. Each button was stamped with the seal of Florida, and the belt buckle was a two-piece design that contained the image of a single palm tree slightly crooked to the side. My wife wanted me to have a proper jacket worthy of my rank.

At the bottom of the trunk were my spurs and Colt dragoon revolvers. They were still in their holsters on the belt. The cap pouch and cartridge box were there as well. I put my clothes and gear on in the room and took a good look at myself in the long mirror. I looked much more like a cowboy from the south Florida frontier—perhaps even somewhat like a pirate with my dark beard. I certainly didn't look like a farmer from the cotton belt.

I closed the trunk, walked over to the wardrobe, and opened both doors. In the back, I found my sword and long gun. The sword was more for decoration. It was made for the state militias and contained the bust of an Indian princess on the handle. I didn't think it would be of much use, so I left it. The state had a poor supply of weapons, and I preferred my own. I was a fan of Colt, and I always tried to update my weapons with the times. My long gun was a new Colt revolving rifle. Between my revolvers and the long gun, I had 18 shots before I had to reload everything. I closed the wardrobe doors.

I exited the room with my gear and began to head down the stairs when my wife exited the room she had entered earlier. I stopped halfway down the stairs. She paused and looked at me.

"The transformation is amazing," Faith said. "South Florida made you sinful, and now you even look the part."

"It's a rough land all around, hummingbird," I said.

I took a deep breath, shook my head slightly, and put my arms up slightly for a moment. I felt like giving up on explaining, but I would try it again.

"I'm not going to south Florida," I said again.

"Liar!" she replied. "You go get on your way before your friends leave you. We'll take care of ourselves."

"You don't understand," I said. "I don't have a choice."

"Really?" she began. "Is that what you told yourself when you did all that boozing and carousing? How many women were you with when you were on your campaigns?"

"You're right," I said. "I should have never given into temptation."

"And I bet you do it again," she said sternly. "Here, take it."

She held her right arm out. It was the Allen pepperbox pistol she had bought me. It was a dragoon style with a spur trigger guard. I reached out and took the weapon.

"I regret buying that damn thing for you. I bought it in case you needed something as a last resort. I wanted you to come home safely. It just made you a monster."

I was just letting her talk at that point. "What do you mean?"

"I heard the stories. You solved all of your problems at the end of a barrel. How many duels were you in because someone said something about you and you lost your temper? I bet you used that very gun too. You can't solve all your problems at the end of a barrel."

I didn't say anything. How could I? She was right.

It got quiet before I spoke. "Some of my past decisions still haunt me. I wish I could go back and change some of the things I've done. I want nothing more but to grow old with you and be a father to our boys."

"Well, you're not coming back until you change your ways. And from what I've seen, that's not happening anytime soon. When you get to south Florida, you'll revert to your old ways of boozing, having fun in the bordellos, and dueling to prove how tough you are when you are not fighting the Seminoles. I bet...I know...you can't avoid any of it."

"Honey, I promise you I'm not heading to the peninsula."

"You say that, but you always end up in that part of the state. The sirens are calling."

I put my head down and slowly walked down the stairs and out of the house. Faith slammed the door shut. I paused on the porch for a moment and wondered if there was anything else I could do. Then I heard her in the front bedroom. I looked through the glass and lace curtain and saw her lying face down on the bed. It sounded like she was sobbing into her pillow. I waited a few minutes to see if she would come back out, but she never did. I picked up my gear, walked off the porch back down the brick walkway, and closed the gate behind me. The familiar screech from the gate signaled that I had exited the yard.

I loaded my gear onto my horse, untied it, and mounted. I paused once more and looked at the house. Deep down, I was hoping she would come out of the house to stop me, but I knew she wouldn't. I directed my horse to start heading back into town.

~ 3 ~

My horse slowly walked back toward town as I gathered my thoughts after the encounter with my wife. I was deep in thought and paid little attention to my surroundings. As we got closer to town, the farms on the outskirts of town were replaced with wooden buildings of homes and storefronts.

As I entered an older section of town, I directed my horse to stop in front of a boarding house. I dismounted, tied my horse to the hitching post, and walked up the stairs and inside the front entrance.

"Ethan," announced an older woman. "It's been a long time."

It was Eden, or Miss Eden to others; she was the owner of the boarding house and a former prostitute. She was also an old friend. She was older and had a tired look on her face—probably not out of the norm for someone who had to operate a boarding house and a bordello across the street while, at the same time, keeping the peace between drunk cowboys, politicians, and her staff. Despite her busy schedule, she was still dressed to the nines, as always. She was wearing a white and maroon cotton dress with a hoop skirt and ankle boots.

I tipped my hat to be polite, "Good afternoon, Eden."

"Ethan," Eden replied, "I'm glad to see you, but I hope no one recognizes you. You know how quick word travels. I wouldn't want Faith to find out you were here."

"I'll be quick," I said. "I'm looking for Aiden. Is he upstairs in his room?"

"No, he's across the street."

"Figures, the little horny SOB."

Eden grinned as I started to head back out the door.

"Ethan, wait! Let me go in there and get him. You don't need the gossip."

"Eden, it doesn't matter. She thinks I practically live here."

I tipped my hat to Eden and walked out the door, across the boardwalk, and across the muddy street. Once across the street, I crossed the opposing boardwalk and entered the bordello. There was a homely looking girl about 20 years old who approached me.

I jumped right to the chase. "Where's Aiden Sage?"

The girl was caught off guard for a second. "He's upstairs. First room on the left. Is he wanted?"

"No," I replied. Then I walked up the stairs.

When I arrived at the door, I stopped and hit it with the bottom of my fist three times.

"Aiden," I said. "You in there? It's Ethan."

"Ethan?" I heard him say behind the door. "Give me a sec." I could hear Aiden and a girl whispering.

Aiden cracked open the door and looked out. He was about 20. He was still enjoying his youth and always looking for some excitement to break up the norm. He had served under me during the Seminole War of '55 and still dreamed about another fight with them. He thought he was invincible. "Ethan, what's wrong?"

"Get dressed and meet me downstairs. They're drumming up the militia."

"Really?" he replied. "Seminoles again?"

"No, we have another job. We have to head to St. Marks and bring back a prisoner."

He thought about it for a second and shook his head back and forth as if he were debating if it was a good assignment. "I'll be right down," Aiden said. Then the door swung shut.

I went back into the lobby and waited. After a couple of minutes, Aiden was dressed and making his way down the stairs. He was putting on his hat and carrying his jacket while he talked to the girl he was with upstairs.

"When I'm back, I'll tell you about the battles I was in during the last war with the Seminoles," Aiden replied to the young girl.

She smiled and let him talk as she followed him down the stairs. She was more mature than Aiden. She probably heard the same story each day from her clientele.

Aiden continued his attempt to impress the girl. "I almost lost my life once, you know."

"What happened?" she asked as if she was very interested.

"We were charging a group of Seminoles that had been ransacking some of the homesteaders..."

I interrupted Aiden when he got to the bottom of the steps. "Let's go, lover boy. You can tell her all about it when you get back."

I put my right arm around his shoulder to hurry him out the door.

"I love you, darling," Aiden told the girl on his way out the door.

Once he was out the door and in a more rational state of mind, we both walked across the muddy street.

"Battles?" I started. "Almost died? What have you been telling those girls?"

"I'm a veteran of the Third Seminole War. I'm telling them about my exploits."

I shook my head and smiled. I was probably much like that when I was his age. "I didn't remember any of those skirmishes being like the Battle of Withlacoochee."

We entered the boarding house, and Eden was waiting for us.

"But, what about..." Aiden began.

I didn't feel like debating it, and I cut him off. "Just go get your gear. We have a little bit of a trip ahead of us."

As Aiden disappeared upstairs to get his gear from his room, Eden began to talk. "Ethan, I hope no rumors make it back to Faith."

"Like I said, it doesn't matter," I replied. "I'm already in a lot of trouble."

"I'm sure you two will work it out."

I took a deep breath. "I'm trying."

Aiden came back down the stairs in a blue uniform jacket his mother had sewn for him. He had an old, sheathed dragoon saber attached to his belt. Under his belt was a red sash. He had an old Hall rifle. He also had a percussion pistol in a holster and a couple of saddlebags full of gear on his right shoulder.

"You never returned that rifle to the state?" I asked.

"Not yet. I heard talks about a civil war. I thought I might as well hold onto it. I thought they might make me an officer due to my war experience."

Eden and I just looked at him for a second.

"Just go get your horse and meet me outside."

As Aiden went out the door, I looked at Eden and shook my head. "Believe it or not, he does a good job in the field. He thinks he's a West Point soldier."

"Ethan," Eden replied. "We were all that age at one time." She smiled, "I remember you talking like you were invincible on some of your nightly visits. I just let you talk away."

I smiled. "Well, I hope he outgrows it. I know where he's going to end up if he doesn't."

"Ethan, you may not think it, but you have matured. I know you would make a great husband and father. Deep down, you're a good person. I know you. You just need to win Faith back."

I got quiet for a couple of seconds. "Thank you, Eden. I hope I can."

"All that being said, you need to go quickly." Eden got behind me, put both hands on my back, and began to push me out the door. "If anyone spots you here and tells your wife, she will never let you go back home."

After I exited the building, I crossed the boardwalk, went down the stairs, untied my horse, and mounted it. I waited a couple of minutes when Aiden came around the corner on his horse. I took a good look at him in the light of the cloudy day. He was wearing an old black leather forage cap from the 1830s.

"Aiden, let me buy you a new hat. I'll buy you a hat like mine."

"I'm alright. This is an old uniform hat, just like the dragoons. It's official. We're mounted volunteers like the dragoons, right?"

"Yes, and they wore those hats. I remember them from over 20 years ago. If you continue to wear that hat here in 1858, you're going to get shot by some drunk cowboy. Let me buy you a slouch hat."

"I'm fine. I look like a soldier."

"You stick out like a sore thumb."

I looked at Aiden's face. He was determined to keep it. There was no point in pushing the matter. With that, we set off for the train station.

~ 4 ~

Aiden and I had caught the last train to St. Marks and spent the night in town. I had been here many times for the rail line. The town was normally quiet, but I could tell everyone was still uneasy from the events that had unfolded the night before.

After we arrived, we slept on some cots in the back of the roundhouse. It was more of a wooden barn than a roundhouse, but it still served the same purpose. Aiden was expecting us to stay in a hotel, and he was less than enthusiastic when he found out where I had planned for us to stay. When morning came, Aiden and I headed to the sheriff's office so they could transfer the prisoner to us.

"Morning, deputy," I replied as we walked through the door.

"You must be Major Tucker," the deputy replied.

I was only a captain during the Seminole Wars. The "Major" almost caught me off guard, but I knew what was going on. That was Ryder's way of saying no hard feelings. He was probably hoping it would make me forget about the incident in his office yesterday.

"We were told yesterday you would be coming for our prisoner," continued the deputy.

"That's right," I began. "We're bringing him back to Tallahassee to stand trial. The governor wants to ensure justice is served."

The deputy went to his desk and grabbed a paper and pen. "Just sign this and he's yours." I glanced at the paper. It was a release form signing the prisoner over to me. I signed it and handed it back to the deputy. I heard Aiden behind me checking his guns, preparing for the exchange.

The deputy continued to talk as he placed the form on top of his desk. He reached into a drawer and pulled out a cell key. "His name is Alaster Conley. He hasn't talked all night, but he's quick with a gun. I got his name from a ranch foreman. His boss bought some cattle from him when he arrived. He killed our sheriff before he shot that gambler. There were some other men with him, but they scattered sometime in the night after the trouble started in the saloon."

Aiden and I followed the deputy toward the cell. Another man was sitting in a chair in front of the cell with a long rifle lying in his lap. He was closely monitoring the prisoner. Alaster was lying on the cot with his legs propped up against the cell bars. His arms were folded, and his hat was tilted down in front of his face to block the light from his eyes so he could sleep.

"Alaster," said the deputy.

Alaster didn't move.

"Alaster!" repeated the deputy. He kicked the cell door at the same time.

Alaster slowly tilted his hat back and looked at us.

"Your escort is here," said the deputy. "They are taking you to Tallahassee."

Alaster slowly put his boots on the ground and sat up like a serpent examining its prey. He stood up and walked over to the cell door. He examined Aiden and me then gave a quick smirk. He turned back around, slowly walked toward the cot at the back of the cell, and lit a cigarette like he was pondering. He turned and slowly walked back toward the cell door while he shook the match in his hand to put it out. He took a puff of the tobacco, inhaled, and blew the smoke from his nose. "Well, let's go," Alaster replied with an uncomforting smile.

The deputy opened the cell door, placed the handcuffs on him, and turned him over to us. We told the deputy goodbye and exited the building. As we led Alaster down the street toward the train station, I decided to talk with him.

"Mr. Conley," I began. "I don't want to be here anymore than you do. If you just cooperate with us, I won't give you a hard time. It's a two-hour ride straight to town. Why don't you just enjoy it?"

Alaster didn't say a word. He just followed along in his handcuffs. He seemed quite relaxed for a man that was going to be hung.

The engineers had begun fueling the firebox early in the morning, and it was ready to go, judging from the deep breathing noises radiating from the locomotive. The engine was a typical 4-4-0 type pulling a few house cars. Our horses were already loaded on a flat car at the very end of the train. Second to the end was the way car. We were going to ride in there with some of the railroad workers. The house cars were empty, and the train was heading back to pick up another load of cotton.

As we approached, the train conductor slid the door open on the way car. His clothes were covered in soot, and he was missing two fingers on his left hand. I had seen him from time to time when I had to work on the rail line, but I didn't know him. Aiden and I climbed up into the car, both of us keeping a hand on our prisoner. Once inside, we stood up, pulling Alaster into the car with us. The conductor helped lift Alaster.

I looked around the way car. It was basically a house car with four windows cut into the sides. The workers had placed some cots along the walls, and there was a stove in the corner with a chimney heading toward the roof.

"Come on, Aiden," I said.

We both pulled Alaster along by his upper arms like a disobedient child. We sat him down on the floor with his back to the wall. Aiden and I sat down on each side of him. We placed our hats in our laps, and Aiden placed Alaster's hat in his lap. We heard the train whistle blow twice and then a release of steam. The engine began to chug slowly. The link and pin couplers began to jerk the cars one by one as they stretched tight. Once the train was stretched out completely, we were on our way back home.

"I'll be glad when we get back," I said.

Alaster didn't say anything. He just looked out the open door of the car. The railroad workers sometimes left the doors open to let the heat out. Today was no exception. It was a hot and humid day—fine weather for the cotton belt.

"This wasn't much of a mission," Aiden said.

"Count your blessings," I replied.

We both had to raise our voices over the noises of the train.

Then we both got quiet. I could feel a slight breeze from the open door. It was very comfortable. I crossed my legs, folded my hands on my chest, and decided to enjoy my ride back.

~ 5 ~

Aloud explosion in the distance rattled the way car. I put both my hands flat on the floor and uncrossed my legs. I looked over at Aiden, and he looked at me. Alaster didn't move. He just stared at the opposite wall of the car with his hands folded on his stomach.

The wheels of the locomotive shrieked to a stop, and the link and pin couplers of the cars began to slam against one another and travel toward the back of the train like dominoes. When the sound got close, the way car slammed against the house car in front of us. We all fell forward, and the car came to a complete stop, with the flat car behind us slamming into our car. The horses began to neigh as they fell forward with the motion of the train. We picked ourselves up off the floor and looked around. The railroad workers in the car were just as confused as us. Aiden and I held tight onto Alaster's arms.

Another loud explosion behind the train rattled the walls of the way car. The various tools hanging on the walls clanged as they swung against one another. Debris rained down on the roof of the car.

The train conductor climbed in via the roof and looked at me. "There are three riders out there! They blew up the track in front of the train and at the rear. That last blast blew up the flat car behind us. I'm afraid you've lost all your horses."

Everything got silent except for the locomotive breathing deeply. The sound of horses galloping broke the silence as three rough-looking cowboys rode up to the open doors of the way car. I pulled out my revolver and placed it against Alaster's head.

One of the riders dismounted and climbed into the car. He was wearing a dark poncho, torn pants, and brogans with spurs. His slouch hat was black with dried sweat stains.

"Mister," began the rider. "Unless you want me to start shooting the railroad workers, I suggest you put that gun down. You're outnumbered here."

I looked over at the railroad workers. They had their hands up and were scared. I looked over at Aiden; he had his rifle pointed at the rider. The other cowboys were armed with revolvers but had rifles drawn for the moment. In any other place, I would have shot Alaster and started shooting at the cowboys. This time was different. Innocent people were in the way, and I needed to bring back Alaster alive. If something happened to him, I knew the adjutant general would retaliate. This whole assignment was probably another way for him to impress the governor.

"Put your gun down, Aiden," I replied.

"But sir..." Aiden replied.

"Put it down," I said. "I don't want these workers to get killed. Alaster isn't worth it."

"Yes," replied the rider. "Listen to him. Put the gun down, boy."

Aiden lowered his rifle.

"Hand me the keys," continued the rider.

I handed the rider the keys, and he undid Alaster's handcuffs.

"Sorry it took so long, boss," replied the rider.

"Quite alright," replied Alaster. He was putting his hat on his head. "I was beginning to think you boys weren't going to show. Take their guns. I need them."

The rider looked at me. "Hand them over, mister. Give them to Mr. Conley."

The mounted cowboys pointed their guns right at us. Aiden and I handed over our weapons. I began to hand over the pepperbox pistol when Alaster laughed.

"What the hell is that!" Alaster replied. "Keep it."

The other cowboys smiled.

Alaster armed himself with my Colt rifle and revolvers. He gave Aiden's weapons to one of the mounted cowboys. "Well, boys, it would appear that the four horsemen ride again. It's been fun, but we have a boat to catch in Pensacola."

Alaster and the rider jumped out of the car and mounted their horses. The outlaws had brought an extra horse for Alaster.

Aiden, the railroad workers, and I ran to the door. We watched as the outlaws took off west and disappeared into the thick woods of the Florida panhandle.

"Why'd you let them go?" asked Aiden.

"Not now, Aiden," I replied.

"You never let anyone go before," Aiden continued. "You always fought tooth and nail."

"Aiden," I replied, "again, this time, it's different." I pointed toward the railroad workers. "Before, I didn't have to worry about any civilians getting killed. Our ultimate job is to protect them."

Aiden got quiet. I looked at the conductor. "Is everyone else okay?"

"I think so," he replied.

"We need to get this train moving," I said urgently. "We need to get some horses so we can go after them."

~ 6 ~

The conductor went right to work to get the train moving. He wasted no time. There were spikes, spike pullers, shovels, and various other tools hanging on the walls of the way car. He began taking them down and passing them out to the railway workers, Aiden, and me. He grabbed a couple of extra tools for himself. "Come on," he said. "There's no time to waste."

We all climbed out of the car and followed the conductor toward the front of the train. One of the workers had climbed out of the locomotive cab to help. The engineer stayed behind to keep an eye on the boiler.

The track rails were a mangled mess, and the ties were blown out of the bed of gravel where the outlaws had placed the dynamite.

"Undo those plates connecting the rails to the damaged line and pull up those spikes," the conductor said. The workers began undoing the bolts. He pointed at Aiden and me. "Start moving those crossties out of the way." Aiden, another worker, and I began digging up and removing the damaged ties. The damaged parts were tossed to the side.

The conductor led us to the back of the train. Another worker was uncoupling the remains of the flat car. Flies were beginning to find the remains of our horses. Once we got past the damaged flat car, the conductor spoke. "Let's take these four rails apart and begin moving them toward the front of the train." He looked at me. "How many crossties were damaged?"

"Just two. The others are fine. They have been reburied and are ready for the new rails."

The conductor spoke to two other workers. "Help them dig out two ties and bring them to the front."

After we dug out two crossties, we began moving the first one to the front of the train. The other workers were already fastening the first set of rails when we got there. We placed the tie down and ran back to get the other. On our return, the first crosstie was being laid into place. We placed the other tie and packed it in the gravel. After about 30 minutes, the rails in front of the train were fixed.

With the obstruction cleared, we loaded back onto the train and hung the tools back on the walls of the way car. Two short whistles blasted out from the locomotive, and the train began to roll—the couplers stretching tight like before. I looked out the open way car. The conductor stood by the track as he waved the train to slowly pass over the patch as he kept an eye on it. When the way car passed, he climbed onto the ladder heading to the roof. He then made his way toward the locomotive.

When we neared the station in Tallahassee, I could see that the platform was full of people. News traveled fast. They wanted to find out more about what happened. The locomotive gave one short whistle and came to a stop at the station. Aiden and I exited the train and made our way through the crowd. A couple of reporters from the local paper attempted to ask us about what happened, but we ignored them.

Without our horses, we had no choice but to walk to the adjutant general's office. When we arrived, I walked into the office, and Aiden waited outside on the boardwalk.

I saw the secretary. "I need to talk with Ryder," I said. "We need to hurry." I didn't even bother with formalities.

The secretary didn't say anything. He hurried to the back. After a few seconds, the secretary came back, with Ryder trailing behind.

"Ethan, what happened?" Ryder began. "Where's the prisoner?"

"He had a gang waiting for us," I replied. "They were prepared for us. They stopped the train with explosives and took him."

"That prisoner is supposed to be here today," Ryder replied. He didn't even think about asking if we were okay. It never even crossed his mind. "I promised the governor he would be here today."

"They killed our horses and took our guns. They also did a lot of damage to the railroad."

"Why didn't you fight back?"

"They said they would retaliate by killing the railroad workers if I had done so."

"Where are the outlaws at now?"

"They began riding west. Alaster said they were heading for Pensacola to catch a ship."

The adjutant general paused for a moment and thought about his options. "I can't believe you let them go," he said.

I didn't say anything. That just meant he was going to throw me to the wolves to protect his hide. "Look, the longer we wait, the more distance they are putting between us."

Ryder thought about it for a minute, "What do you need from me?"

"Aiden and I need some horses and weapons. Some extra cash might help too. I'm not sure how long we'll be gone."

"How long will it take you to get to Pensacola?"

"It'll take us a few days. We'll try to move as fast as we can."

~ 7 ~

Traffic on the railroad had come to a standstill for the entire day. As news spread about the escaped fugitive and the commotion on the railroad, more townspeople began to gather at the station to see if they could find out more gossip.

The state had managed to drum up a couple of old Hall rifles and a few percussion pistols for Aiden and me. We were also able to borrow a few quarter horses from some friends. Ryder was afraid to go to the governor and ask for extra funds to finance the venture, so we left with the money we had from before.

Once we got back to the railway station, the railroad workers had two house cars hitched behind the tender and a flat car trailing behind full of parts to repair the rail line. As soon as Aiden and I arrived, the railroad workers quickly loaded our horses into the second house car. Instead of a way car or passenger car, Aiden, the railroad workers, several slaves owned by the railroad, and I rode in the first house car. The railroad thought it would offer more protection against any possible marksmen waiting to take a shot at us. Inside the cab of the locomotive were two deputies armed with rifles ready to return fire—probably an arrangement made between the sheriff and the owners of the railroad.

As soon as we boarded the train, we were off. The new owners of the railroad were urgently wanting to get the line back to full operation. This would have never been the case with the previous owners. It worked great for Aiden and me.

The house car doors were closed with a small crack for ventilation. It was just enough for me to peek my head out and see the track ahead of the locomotive. The trip was much quicker this time. Each station or way stop was full of locals hoping to get more news on the outlaws.

After about 30 minutes, I could see the damaged track coming into view. The locomotive slowed and screeched to a stop, with the house cars and flat car all slamming forward against the tender. Everyone paused for a moment. All that could be heard were the sounds of the locomotive breathing. Some of the workers and slaves looked through spaces between the planks of the car, searching for gunmen in the woods. They were nervous about what was going to happen the moment the doors swung open. I peeked out the door and could see the mangled track and damaged flat car. The remains of our horses were covered in a blanket of flies by this point. I glanced over the woods where the outlaws rode off. I didn't see one sign of them.

The train whistle blew four short blasts in a row. The railroad worker standing next to me tapped me on the shoulder. "That's our cue. The deputies say it's clear."

The railroad workers slung the doors of the house car open and went right to work like ants scouring a nest that had just been disturbed. A plank was pulled from the flat car and placed at the west side of the second house car. They led our horses out of the car. As Aiden and I mounted our horses, the workers and slaves had already begun moving the damaged flat car off to the side.

I looked at the woods and found the tracks where Alaster and his men rode off.

"Let's go, Aiden," I said. "We're losing daylight."

We directed our horses into the woods, following the path of the outlaws. I took one glance behind me. The railroad slowly disappeared out of sight and was replaced by the thick woods of pine, oak, and palmettos. I could just make out the train and the workers running back and forth between the flat car at the end of the train and the tracks in front of the locomotive. I could hear the slaves in sequence as they began digging out the damaged crossties. After a few minutes, the sights and sounds of the railroad were replaced with the natural beauty of the Florida Panhandle and the sounds of its inhabitants. Casitas and birds sang in the afternoon sun as it tried to peek through the thick trees. Crickets got quiet as we passed on our horses, the silence only disturbed by a small creature disturbing the brush in the near distance.

After a couple of hours, the trail from the outlaws stopped. It looked as if they let their horses walk around in circles and on top of one another's tracks. Then they took off in two directions.

"Sir, look," Aiden said. He pointed at another set of tracks.

"They split up," I said. "You follow those tracks, and I will follow the ones over here. If you have any issues, fire your gun. Be careful. They could be watching us right now."

"Yes sir," replied Aiden, just like a good soldier.

We parted ways. Some spots of the tracks looked as if they had begun to dry. They had passed through here hours ago, but one thing was certain. They had turned to the north. By the early evening, I saw a rider heading my way. It was Aiden.

"You alright, Aiden?"

"Yes, sir. I just followed the tracks, and they led me here."

My horse walked a few more feet, and the trails merged into one.

"It's hard to cover tracks in this mud," I began. "It's been raining for days. I think they tried to throw us off, but they must've given up."

I looked around in the fading light of the day, the thick trees still blocking most of the light. They had managed to walk their horses in circles, like before. This time, they all changed direction and rode off together.

"They changed directions again," I said.

"Where do you think they are heading?" asked Aiden.

The tracks were heading southeast toward the bend. The argument my wife and I had yesterday came back to me instantly. They were heading for a land that could make the most honest man corrupt. Sometimes out of want, sometimes just for survival—I had been there several times and vowed never to return, but my wife was right. I was being drawn back to it.

"They're heading for the frontier."

~ 8 ~

Days turned into weeks before we found any sign of the outlaws. Aiden and I had been traveling fast each day and camping at night. We passed through a couple of settlements, and they claimed to have seen four men matching the descriptions of the outlaws. At some point along the way, they had turned east.

As we approached the New River, there was an old log cabin shack coming into view. I knew the inhabitants. There was a man there married to a Seminole woman with two kids. He was operating a ferry across the river.

When we arrived, a tall man with blue eyes and a dark complexion stood up out of a chair on the porch and looked at me. He was wearing a button-down shirt with a vest, cotton trousers, and knee-high officer boots. After he stood up, he put a light slouch hat on top of his head.

"It's been a long time," I said.

"About a year now," he replied.

Aiden didn't say anything.

"Riley," I began. "You still telling people you're half Spanish."

"More or less," replied the tall man. He stepped off the porch and approached me. He was actually half Irish and half Seminole. He never met his father, but the rumor was he was an Irish deserter when the British owned Florida. He began living with the Seminoles shortly before the Spanish took control of Florida. He never knew his last name, but everyone called him Riley. He was raised by his mother. I fought him in the last two Seminole Wars. We respected each other as fighters. When the Seminoles were rounded up after the war of '55, Riley managed to slip away with his family. I never told anyone about his whereabouts.

"I'm looking for some men," I said. "A man named Alaster is their leader. He killed a couple of people in St. Marks, and I'm supposed to bring him back to Tallahassee." I gave descriptions of the cowboys. "Have you seen them?"

"I saw the men about a day ago. I gave them passage. They were heading toward Starke."

"Want to make some money?" I asked.

"What do you need?"

"I think these cowboys may be heading for south Florida. I need a scout."

"How much?"

"Average monthly wage of a foot soldier?"

"I don't know," he replied. "They were a rowdy bunch. They didn't care too much for me."

"What if I pay you $15.00?"

He was still hesitant. I knew he would be hard to convince.

"Are you heading for Tallahassee anytime soon?"

"I might."

I had depleted the money that Ryder had given me. I looked in my wallet. "I have $20 from the Tallahassee Railroad Company. They have a pretty good store."

He thought about it.

"That's $35.00, Riley. That's not bad."

Aiden was eyeing the cash.

"I want the $35.00 and something else," Riley replied.

"What's that?" I asked.

"I want to be a soldier in the militia."

"What?"

"I want to be a soldier in the militia. Can you put in a word for me?"

"Riley, if they find out I recommended a Seminole for the militia, they'll hang me from a tree in front of the capitol."

"Don't tell them I'm part Seminole."

Aiden looked at me with a shocked look on his face.

"Tell them I'm part Spanish. Tell them my last name is Hernandez, like your major general in the war of '35. They don't need to know the truth."

I could tell he was determined. Deep down, I knew he didn't have a chance. I wasn't sure if he wanted to prove something to himself, if he was hoping for acceptance in our society, or if he just liked the lifestyle of a warrior. I paused before I answered. "I'll see what I can do."

He looked at his two sons. "Can you operate the ferry for your mother while I'm gone?"

His oldest son, maybe 15, spoke very assured of himself. "I can. I'll take charge."

Riley looked back at me. "Let me get my gear and saddle my horse."

As Riley walked off, Aiden began to ask me questions.

"Sir, who is that?"

"He's an honorable adversary. I fought him in the Seminole War of '35, and you may not know it, but he scouted for the Seminoles in the war of 1855."

"Do you trust him?"

"He sticks to his word. Don't be mistaken; he would fight us tooth and nail if the Seminoles went on the warpath again. He's probably acting as a lookout for the remaining Seminoles to the south. But we respect one another as soldiers. We also need him. He's very knowledgeable about the terrain of the peninsula."

"We removed all of the Seminoles," Aiden replied.

"Don't kid yourself. I guarantee you there are some diehards hiding out in the Glades."

After Riley mounted his horse, his sons helped all three of us cross the New River on the ferry. When we exited the ferry, Riley waved goodbye to his family, and we continued down the path toward Starke.

"Aiden," I said. "Scout ahead for a little bit. I want to talk with Riley."

"Yes sir," Aiden replied. He hurried ahead a little bit to scout the road in front of us.

"He's still wearing that hat?" asked Riley.

"I tried to buy him a slouch hat so he wouldn't stick out."

"I remember him wearing that hat during the last war. It was an easy marker."

"I know."

"Some drunken cow hunter is going to shoot him if he doesn't get rid of that hat."

"I know."

"Did things ever improve between you and your wife?"

"We're still fighting. I'm trying to improve my ways. She says I still like to spend too much time away from home. She still gets all over me for my drinking and carousing when I was younger and getting into duels. She doesn't want me around my boys."

"Still reading that scripture?"

"Yes. I'm reading about the Book of Job now."

"The Book of Job?" Riley asked. "What's it about?"

"From what I can gather, Job is a God-fearing man who is challenged by Satan to give up his faith."

"Did he give it up?"

~ 9 ~

The evening was approaching fast as the three of us continued to trail the renegades. As we approached the settlement of Starke, I could hear a very familiar sound.

"Ugh," I began, "not more railroads."

Aiden and Riley looked at me briefly as we stopped our
horses and took in the sight. Just beyond the clearing of the
trees, the trail led us to the settlement. The sight we witnessed
was a mixture of wooden shacks and tents. Just ahead of the
city was a freshly laid track. In front of the track was a foreman
directing slaves. They were laying crossties for the next set of
rails. Right at the center of the town was a locomotive with several freight cars and a way car. I read about this rail line in the
paper. It was the Florida Railroad Company making its way to
Cedar Keys.

As we directed our horses into the makeshift settlement,
two men caught my attention. Aiden and Riley noticed them
too. Riley didn't say anything. He was a naturally quiet but ob-
servant man. He liked to take note and figure things out.

"Sir," Aiden said, "look over there."

Two lawmen were talking with a couple of railroad workers.
The lawmen were on horseback, and the railroad workers were
standing in the door of the way car. The foreman wandered
over and leaned against the rail car so he could hear the con-

versation. I turned my horse in their direction. Aiden and Riley followed.

"Evening," I said. "I'm Major Tucker of the Florida Militia. Did something happen here?"

The conductor spoke first. "Our train was robbed by four outlaws. Two climbed on board, pointed guns at the engineer, and told him to stop the train. Once we came to a stop, the other two outlaws appeared, entered our way car, and stole the payroll."

"It might be the same guys we're going after," I said. "Their leader was supposed to go to court in Tallahassee, but his gang saved him on his way to trial. Have you seen them before?"

The sheriff spoke up, "This is the first time we've dealt with them. It's usually quiet through here."

"We didn't get a good look at them," replied the conductor. "They were wearing bandanas over the lower portion of their faces."

I gave them a description of Alaster's attire and his height.

"That matches one of them," said the other railroad worker. "As a matter of fact, he was giving them orders. He was one of the latter two riders who showed up after the train stopped."

"Sounds like we're getting close," Aiden said.

"When did this happen?" I asked.

"A few hours ago," responded the conductor. "They're long gone."

"Did you see what direction they were heading?" I asked.

"They were heading due south."

There was a crowd of people surrounding us at this point. I looked at the foreman. "Did you or anyone see these riders pass through? Did any strangers wander into town?"

"I don't know," replied the foreman. "I was busy with the slaves."

I looked at the crowd. "Did any of you see any strangers come through?"

The crowd got quiet.

I looked at Aiden and Riley. "At least we know we're on the right trail. Let's go."

I mounted my horse and began to direct it outside of town when Aiden stopped me.

"Sir," Aiden said, "we haven't eaten all day. We need to do something."

"Since you guys are going after the men who robbed our pay," began the foreman, "the least we can do is feed you." He pointed to a tent. "Why don't you head to the mess tent and get a bite to eat before you leave? Besides, it looks like it's about to rain. You won't get far in bad weather."

I looked in the distance and could see a storm approaching. The lightning lit up the sky as it approached.

"Thank you kindly," I responded. "I guess we will eat first and let the weather pass."

We dismounted from our horses and watered them. A stable worker working for the rail line offered to feed them. We thanked him, headed into the mess tent, and sat down at a table to eat. During supper, we talked.

"If I were an outlaw," Riley began, "I would be heading for south Florida too."

"Why do you say that?" I asked.

"North Florida, Georgia, and the deep south are basically settled. I don't see any place for them to go. I'm sure there are wanted posters all over those areas."

"I can see that," I replied.

"Once they get past Pine Level," Riley continued, "they are free. There is no organized law down there. A few sheriffs on horseback, but they are not going to venture outside their jurisdictions. Depending on how far south they go, they may never be found."

"Like those Seminoles, right?" I asked with a smile.

Riley wasn't sure how to respond. He didn't say anything.

"I think they will be found," I said. "It's just a matter of time. They are not good at lying low. They stir up too much trouble wherever they go."

After we ate, Aiden left to check on the horses. It was raining, and the thunder was rolling across the sky like an angry giant. The only thing separating us from the environment outside was the thin layer of the tent. I didn't know why Aiden decided to check on the horses, but there was no point in trying to tell him otherwise. Riley and I decided to enjoy some tobacco while we waited for the storm to pass. I lit my pipe, and Riley lit a cigarette.

After a few minutes, a railroad worker walked up to us. "May I have a seat?"

We didn't say anything. I was in the middle of inhaling my pipe. I waved my hand to the empty chair as a sign of agreement. He sat down.

"Are you the famous Captain Tucker?" he asked.

"I guess I am," I replied. "I don't know about famous."

"On the contrary," he replied, "I know you."

"How's that?" I asked.

"I was a private during the Seminole War of '35. No one ever put you down."

My past was coming back to haunt me—the very same thing that got me in trouble with my wife.

"How many duels were you in?" asked the railroad worker. He would not stop. "You never lost one! No one dared mess with you."

I didn't say anything. Riley sat quietly, smoking his cigarette.

"You're right," I said. I pulled out the pepperbox gun that my wife gave me and laid it on the table. "I used this gun in some of those fights." I wasn't trying to start anything. I was hoping I appeased him so he would just go away. It didn't work.

"Let's have a drink," he replied. The railroad man pulled out a bottle of whiskey from his jacket. "I heard you were a drinker too. I'm Irish. I bet I can drink you under this table!"

He took a swig of the bottle, wiped his lower lip with his sleeve, and placed the bottle in front of me on the table. I smiled, grabbed the bottle with my right hand, picked it up, and looked at the worker.

"I beg to differ," I replied. "I can outdrink you easily." Then I paused and stopped smiling. I reflected for a minute. I thought about my wife and the conversation we had before I left Tallahassee. Some of the duels I participated in were a result of my drinking.

Riley continued to watch.

"But not today," I said. I put the bottle back down. "I have a job to do."

"Not even for an old war buddy?" asked the worker.

I took a deep breath. "Not today," I said. I handed the bottle back to him, and he put it away. I put my gun away.

"Maybe the next time you pass through?" he asked.

I hesitated before I answered. "I probably won't be back. I'm looking to settle down."

The railroad worker stood up and reached out to shake my hand. I shook it. "It was still a pleasure to meet you," he said. "We showed those Seminoles something, didn't we?" Then he walked off.

Riley and I got quiet for a minute. I knew Riley was thinking about what the worker said, not that he would say anything to me.

"I thought you were going to give in for a second," Riley responded.

"Almost," I said. "I was thinking about it."

"What made you stop?" he asked.

"I thought about my wife," I said.

"That's what I thought," Riley said. He leaned over to me. "You just keep that thought of her and your kids in the back of your mind. Any time you want to give up, just think of them. It will get you through anything."

"You know this," I asked.

"How do you think I got through those wars?" Riley asked. He leaned back in his chair and took another puff of his cigarette.

After a couple of minutes, Aiden entered the tent. He looked at me. "The storm is letting up. Do you want to head out?"

"It's already getting dark," I said. "Let's spend the night here, and we'll get a fresh start in the morning."

~ 10 ~

Before we left the town the following morning, I wrote two letters detailing our trip. I sent one to Faith and the other to Ryder. As we began heading south and the days rolled by, the cotton and sugar plantations began to fade away, being replaced with the open ranges yet to be settled by the encroaching cattle ranchers and homesteaders. It wasn't long before we came across our next possible sign of the outlaws. We stopped our horses and took in the sight.

"No doubt another conquest by the horsemen," replied Aiden.

A stagecoach had been robbed. Riley and I dismounted from our horses and slowly approached. The driver was leaning back in his seat, lifeless. He appeared to have taken a shot from a rifle. The passengers were in no better condition. There were three of them, all of whom had been shot at close range.

"Could be," I replied. "Could be other outlaws too."

"Why do you think they killed them?" asked Aiden. He was still mounted on his horse.

"They probably got a good look at their faces," I responded.

Riley opened the door and took a look inside the stage. He covered his lower face with his handkerchief as he examined the bodies. The flies buzzed around as each body was disturbed.

"They've been robbed of their valuables," Riley said.

I began checking out the front of the coach. "It looks like they had four horses hitched," I replied. "They might try to sell them in a town nearby."

"Judging from the state of the bodies," Riley began, "this happened a few days ago."

"They could be heading for that trading post north of Lake Tohopekaliga," I said.

"Possible," Riley replied. "That place is turning into a cow town. Nothing there but cowboys and outlaws. That would certainly be their element."

"If anything," I said, "we can report the incident."

Riley, Aiden, and I found a couple of small shovels in a box on the stage. We took our time and gave the individuals a proper burial as best we could. When we finished, we began our trip south to the trading post.

As we approached the town, we were greeted with the sight of a dead oak tree with a couple of crows cawing. The field itself was full of small red flowers. Hanging from the tree was a man dressed in raggedy clothing with a sign hanging around his neck. It read, "Convicted horse thieves will be treated accordingly."

We stopped our horses on the road.

"Is this legal?" asked Aiden.

"Depends on who you ask," I replied.

We continued into the town, putting the scene behind us. Years ago, this town was nothing more but a trading post. Now, it had grown into a cattle town. Cowboys were moving cattle through the streets, with dogs ensuring the cattle stayed together. The cow hunters, as they were called, would occasionally crack a whip to keep the cattle moving or keep them together.

The town itself consisted of cabins and shacks. Some were saloons, restaurants, stores, and a couple of bordellos—anything to serve this growing community.

I stopped my horse in front of one of the saloons. A couple of rough-looking cowboys with low, hanging slouch hats were sitting in chairs on the boardwalk watching the cattle pass down the street. One was leaning back in his chair with a beer.

"Excuse me," I began. "Is this any law here?"

"Just us mainly," he replied. He took a sip of his beer.

"I guess you guys hung that man outside of town?" I asked.

"No sir," he replied. "I doubt many of us would have gone through the trouble of even making the sign. That was the Spaniard's idea. He's kind of the law around here, I guess."

"Luis?" I asked.

"That's him," replied the cowboy.

"Where's he at?"

"He lives in that cabin across the street." He tilted his head in the direction of a one-room cabin with a porch.

"Thank you kindly," I replied.

I directed my horse across the street after the cattle had passed. Riley and Aiden followed.

"You two stay here," I responded.

I dismounted from my horse and tied it to the rail of the porch. I entered the porch and knocked on the door. Luis answered. His hair was thinner on top and turning gray. He had a white shirt on with cotton trousers and brogans. He had suspenders on, but they were dangling down at his sides.

"Ethan?" he asked. "It's been a long time."

"Hello, Luis," I said.

"I never thought I would see you again," he replied. "What brings you here? Are they calling up the militia?"

"I need to report an incident, and I'm looking for some out-laws," I said.

"You've come to the right place," Luis responded.

"I was told you are the law around here."

"In a way," he said. "Some of the townsmen got together when this place started growing. They decided that they needed a sheriff. They reached the conclusion that since I had been here the longest and served in the militia, I would be a great candidate. They went ahead and made me sheriff. I found out the next morning."

"We found a stagecoach north of here," I began. "It was robbed. I wanted to report it."

"Probably the man we hung," Luis replied. "He tried to sell four horses in town. He thought he could change the brand."

"We buried the passengers and driver," I replied. "They had been dead for a few days."

"Damn it!" I continued. "I thought it might have been done by the men we were tracking."

"Who are you looking for?" Luis asked.

I explained the situation and gave descriptions of the men.

"I know these men," replied Luis. "I had a run-in with Alaster just last night. He was in the saloon."

"When did they leave?"

"I don't believe they have. They were in the bordello last I heard."

I looked at Aiden and Riley. They both looked at me.

"Come on," replied Luis. "I'll take you there."

Luis put on his hat and slid his suspenders up around his shoulders. He grabbed a loaded revolving rifle he had hidden by the door. Riley and Aiden dismounted from their horses and tied them to the post. Then they checked their weapons.

I grabbed my rifle from my saddle and checked my pistols. We followed Luis to the bordello.

We stopped out front of the bordello and stood in the middle of the street. It was a two-story building that stood alone—much nicer than the other places in town. It was probably a kit bought from a catalog.

"There is one exit out back," Luis said. "They might make a run for it."

"Riley, Aiden, go cover it," I said.

Riley and Aiden took off behind the building to keep an eye on the door. I stood close to Luis' side to guard the front.

"Luis," I said. "What are you going to do?"

"I'm going to call them out."

"Luis," I began. "These are some bad dudes. I think we should surprise them."

Luis checked his rifle and continued the conversation. "Let's do this out in public. Sometimes they are less willing to cause trouble in the spotlight so they don't draw more attention to themselves."

"Alaster!" yelled Luis, "You still in there?"

Everyone on the boardwalks stopped to see what was happening. Some hurried out of the way for safety.

"Alaster," Luis continued. "It's Ethan! Run for it!"

A shot was fired from a top window and hit Luis in the chest. He fell backward. Another shot rang out and buzzed by my ear.

It was Alaster, for sure. He had my Colt rifle. I grabbed Luis' rifle and hurried for the security of a post in front of the saloon next door. The sounds of bullets hitting the dirt trailed behind me. I could also hear gunfire behind the building. The horsemen were unleashing a wrath of war upon us.

I leaned out from behind the post to get a view. The bordello had its own yard and sat further back from the other buildings along the street. It gave me a clear view of the upstairs windows. Another shot was fired and hit the edge of the post, sending splinters in all directions. I pulled my head back and pulled some splinters from my cheek. I leaned out again. It was my turn to return fire. I fired at a figure in the window. He fell backward. Then things got quiet. I looked over at Luis. He was still in the street, unresponsive to the commotion.

"Aiden! Riley!" I yelled. "How are you holding up?" I didn't hear anything.

I moved away from the post and against the wall of the saloon. I leaned my gun on the corner of the building and slowly peeked around with the barrel of Luis' gun leading the way. Nothing happened.

I decided to move closer to the bordello. I leaned further out to get a better look. It looked clear—as good a time as any. I made a dash to cross the yard. As I left the secure spot, the front door of the bordello swung open briefly. It was Alaster. He fired a bullet in my direction, and a burning sensation overwhelmed my chest as I realized Alaster had hit me. I fell backward. Thinking quickly, I fired my weapon in Alaster's direction, and he ran back inside.

I staggered off back to the secure spot I had left and leaned against the wall of the saloon. I coughed and realized I was coughing up blood. People along the boardwalk had taken cover or run off by this point.

I leaned around the corner of the saloon, ready to fire again. Another shot rang out from a window by the door. Instantly, a burning sensation flowed through my left hand. I dropped the rifle, grabbed my left arm, and fell back onto the boardwalk.

Two cowboys decided to brave the gunfire and exited the saloon. They hurried toward me. As they crouched low, they grabbed my shoulders, pulled me into the safety of the saloon, and laid me flat on the floor. I looked at my left hand as I struggled to breathe. My index finger and middle finger were dangling by just a bit of flesh. The tip of my ring finger was gone. I laid my hand on my chest and passed out.

~ 11 ~

I woke up in a bed. The room was quiet, and no one was present, but it was a well-furnished and maintained room compared to what most of the town had to offer. It was slightly dark, with some light coming through the thin curtains. I could hear it raining lightly outside, with thunder in the far distance.

I started to get up when a sharp pain ran through my chest. I stopped and put my head back on the pillow. I started to explore my chest with my hands, but my left hand was stiff. I pulled it out from the cover and saw that it was wrapped in a thick bandage. I used my right hand to feel around my chest and found my upper body was wrapped tight in a large bandage. I lifted the cover and checked the rest of my body. I was okay and appeared to be wearing a long nightshirt.

A large, heavy man with a white beard and glasses opened the door and walked into the room. "Well," he began, "good morning. I wasn't sure if you were going to come out of it." He was shining a medical tool of some sort.

I was still kind of groggy, "Where am I?"

"This is my practice," he said. "Technically, my home—I'm a doctor here in town." He walked over to the table in front of the window. He opened a bag, put the tool inside, and closed it. "When I heard there was another shootout, I admit I wasn't too keen on patching up some more outlaws. I know I took an oath, but I can't imagine the lives they have taken from others. You, on the other hand, are different. When I found out you were with the state militia and descended upon our little settlement, I hurried down to the saloon to patch you up. Your men helped me bring you back here."

"It's a good thing you were unconscious," he continued. "It made the operating much easier. You lost your index and middle fingers and the tip of your ring finger. Your chest was a different story. I had to dig a little to find the bullet. I got it. You're lucky, too. It didn't hit anything vital. God was watching over you!"

I was still taking everything to the end. "I'm afraid I can't pay you," I said.

"Like I said, I took an oath," the doctor replied. "Besides, you came to take care of some of these outlaws. That's payment in and of itself."

"How long have I been here?" I asked. I started to pull myself up.

"Careful now," the doctor said. He hurried over to my bedside to help me up. The doctor pulled me up in the bed and placed a pillow behind my back so I could sit up straight. "I don't want anything to start bleeding. You've been here for a couple days, drifting in and out of consciousness."

"Where are my men?" I asked.

"They've been staying in my parlor. They're working hard. Riley has been asking around town about the men in the shootout. Aiden has been taking care of your horses and equipment. There's also been a girl checking in on you."

"A girl?" I asked.

"Yes," he replied. "She said she was an old friend." He leaned closer to me and spoke quietly. "I won't say anything. We all have our own secrets." He hit me in the shoulder and smiled.

"Riley is here now," replied the doctor. "I will tell him that you're awake. My wife also made some chicken and dumplings. I would like for you to eat some so you can get your strength back. I'll be back." The doctor turned and exited the room.

Riley walked in a minute later and smiled. "Damn," Riley said, "you're awake." He walked over and sat on a stool next to my bed. "I guess you're going to start bossing us around again."

I struggled to laugh. I was sore. "You might have a couple more days of peace," I replied. Then we paused. "Did you and Aiden get them?"

"No," Riley said. He got serious. "After you went down, they started firing everything they had at us. We didn't get hurt, but they managed to cover us well. They all escaped. I think one of them got brazed."

"At least you two are okay," I said.

The doctor walked in with a bowl of his wife's cooking, a spoon, and a napkin and handed everything to me. He then poured a glass of water and placed it on the table next to me.

"Thank you," I said. I took a bite. "This is good."

"My wife's specialty," replied the doctor.

"They were waiting for us," Riley continued.

I shook my head in agreement as I took another bite of my meal. "Luis sold us out. I bet they paid him off."

"If you're talking about that so-called sheriff," began the doctor, "I wouldn't be surprised. He has a grudge against us Americans. He blames Jackson for chasing the Spanish out. He misses Spanish rule."

The doctor turned and walked back out of the room.

"On a positive note," Riley began, "they left in a real hurry. We scared Alaster and his men. They left a couple of their horses behind. Aiden said one of the horses was carrying your stolen guns."

"Did you see my Colt dragoons?" I asked.

"There were some," he replied.

"What about my rifle?" I asked. "It's a revolving rifle from Colt."

"I didn't see one," he said.

"Alaster probably kept it," I replied. "I think he fired it at me." I paused. "The doc said you were checking around town while I was out."

"That's right," Riley replied.

"Did you find out anything," I asked.

"Everyone seems to be afraid of them. Only a couple people talked. The outlaws come into town every once in a while and stir up trouble. Everyone says they are known cattle rustlers, but no one dares say anything. Rumor is a couple of cowboys disappeared when they tried to put a stop to Alaster's rustling activities." Riley paused. "They are a product of their environment for sure."

"That doesn't help us much," I said.

"No, but this next part does," continued Riley. "It took 20 dollars and some spirit—you can compensate me later—but I managed to get a cowboy to talk. Alaster's ranch is south of Pine Level. He doesn't own the land; they just built a cabin and claimed it as theirs. I know the location because I've been there before."

"Are you sure?" I asked.

"I've been there many times," Riley replied. "He described the landscape to a tee."

"As soon as the doctor gives me the go-ahead," I said, "we'll start heading to Pine Level."

Riley shook his head in agreement and stood up. "I'll tell Aiden the news as soon as he gets back. I'm glad you're getting better. I was getting worried. Just remember your wife and children." Riley turned and walked out of the room.

I finished my meal and placed the bowl on the bedside table. Then I just sat for a minute and gathered my thoughts. I could hear the thunder getting closer. Another minute went by before the door opened again. This time, it was a familiar face from my past. It was Belle Serene. She was known as the "soiled dove" of the trading post. I was a customer during the Seminole War of '35. She closed the door behind her.

"Serene," I said with a smile. "It's been a long time."

"Hello, Ethan," she replied. She smiled back. "It's been a while."

We were both silent for a minute.

"I came as soon as I heard what happened," Serene said. "I couldn't believe you were back in town." She walked over and sat on the side of my bed.

"From what I've been told, I almost didn't make it."

"You looked it," Serene replied. She looked down at the wounds. "We were worried, Ethan."

"I can't believe you're still here," I said. "I thought you would have moved on from this place by now. I remember you talking about how you always wanted to see Savannah."

"This little town is growing," she replied. "There's a fortune to be made."

"It's come a long way from that old trading post," I said.

"Yes, it has," she said. "I still remember those days. I remember you walking into this place when you were about 20. Both hands balled tight into a fist as you walked down the street. You never backed down from a fight. Indians and all."

"I remember," I said with a smile.

"I heard you got married," Serene said.

"That's right," I replied.

"She's a lucky girl. Remember the time you defended my honor? You walked out in the street with that pepperbox ready to fire." Serene giggled a little. Then she leaned over a little and started rubbing her right hand up and down my leg.

I thought about the incident. I was in a drunken state and had managed to talk myself into a duel. I remember hitting my opponent in the shoulder with a single shot. Then I thought about my wife.

Serene started running her hand further up my leg. Her touch was beginning to work on me. She looked down at me with a slight smile. She wanted me to invite her to lie at my side. I bit down on my teeth, fought the urge, and crossed my arms. The bandage on my left hand made the motion awkward. Serene stopped and pulled her hand back. She knew I wasn't going to be enticed.

"We had some good times," I said.

"You love that girl," Serene said, "don't you?"

"Very much," I replied. "My children too."

"She's a lucky girl," Serene replied. She stood up. "I'll never forget those nights."

"Nor will I," I said. "We had some good times for sure. It was always a pleasure."

"Goodbye, Ethan."

"Goodbye, Serene."

Serene turned and exited the room. I never saw her again.

~ 12 ~

A few days had passed before we approached Pine Level, careful to avoid the town. I had heard of it. It had earned a reputation for being untamed. It had become a center for outlaws, gangs, cowboys, and ranchers who often clashed with one another in the streets. It was also Alaster's element, and he, more than likely, knew many of the townspeople. If we were spotted or began asking questions, there was no doubt in my mind it would make it back to Alaster and his gang. We needed to surprise them.

I let Riley lead the way for a couple of days once we passed Pine Level. Aiden and I followed along as he led us through the outer reaches of the Everglades so we could circle back and approach Alaster's ranch from the south. I was also willing to bet it was Riley's old stomping grounds from during the wars. He probably knew where the remaining Seminoles were in the Glades, and he did not want us to accidentally find them.

One day passed as we headed deeper into the woods. We went south, crossed waterways, turned east, and cut our own trails through thick vegetation so our horses could pass. Another day passed before we turned north. Then we crossed more waterways, all while keeping an eye out for alligators and moccasins. Altogether, we spent three days in the Everglades before we started to approach Alaster's ranch.

"We're getting close," Riley said.

"How do you know?" asked Aiden.

"The ground is getting higher," Riley replied. "There's not as much water here."

It was just about dark when I was ready to ask Riley about our location. Before I could get a word out, he stopped us in our tracks.

"Ethan," Riley said. "They should be right beyond those trees.

"Aiden," I said. "Keep an eye on our horses. Try to keep them quiet."

Riley and I slowly approached. We got low and crept past the tree line Riley pointed out and made our way to a fence just beyond the trees. We lay flat on our stomachs to avoid being seen. I pulled out my binoculars and looked. It wasn't much of a sight. There was a single-room cabin with a porch at the front. There was another building. It looked like a makeshift stable for their horses. It was made of logs and tree limbs, just like the fences. They had a few cattle grazing in the fenced areas.

"They probably rustled these cattle from the neighboring ranches we passed a few days ago," I said.

"Probably," Riley responded.

"Let's go back into the woods and circle around to the other side of the property," I said. "Let's get a better view of this cabin."

We went back into the woods and circled back. Then we lay low to the ground and worked our way up to another fence to get a clearer view, just like before.

"It looks like there is a window on each side and a door on the front leading to the porch," I said. "Perfect for an ambush."

"That's exactly what I was thinking," Riley responded. "If we surround it, it's going to be very hard for them to escape."

"I wish the window shutters were open," I said. "We could get an even better view."

A noise from inside the cabin interrupted us. I looked with my binoculars. The front door opened, and Alaster stepped out onto the porch. Two more of his gang followed. Alaster was complaining.

"Look," Alaster told the men. "Just start shooting the damned things. I'm tired of these alligators taking our calves when we water the herd."

"Alaster," one of the outlaws began, "if we do that, another alligator is going to move in and take its territory."

"Then rope it," Alaster said. "Then tie it to a tree or something before the cattle drink. I can't afford to lose anymore. We might have to make a few more nightly runs if this continues."

I looked at Riley.

"Let's get back to Aiden," I said.

Riley and I slowly crawled back to the woods, out of sight of the cabin. We took our time not to make any noise that would catch the outlaws' attention.

When we reached Aiden, we decided to eat some hardtack and jerky and come up with a plan. We couldn't make any coffee, as the light from the fire would give us away.

"I think we have the upper hand this time," I said. "There's one door on the cabin. Unless they decide to jump out a window, which will slow them down, there is no other place for them to go."

"They'll probably try it," Aiden said.

"True," Riley added. "If they get desperate, they will do anything to run."

"Aiden," I said. "There's a makeshift stable there. I want you to approach from behind and use the structure as cover."

"Yes sir," Aiden replied.

"Riley," I said, "can you cover the back of the cabin? Just in case one tries to sneak away into the woods. You know this area best, and I know they can't hide from you."

"They'll be sorry if they try," he replied.

"I'll cover the front door," I said. "When I fire the first shot, we'll try to move in closer to surround the structure."

At that moment, we heard something stirring in the brush around our camp. I grabbed my Colt, and Riley grabbed the handle of his knife. Aiden grabbed his rifle and pointed it in the direction of the commotion. Then, a dog-like figure appeared and froze. We could just make it out in the faint light of the evening. It was a black wolf with its eyes frozen on us. It was as shocked as we were. A few seconds passed before it backed up and left.

"That was odd," Riley said.

"What do you mean?" Aiden asked. "That's not uncommon out here. We're in the woods."

"Listen," Riley replied.

"I don't hear anything," Aiden said.

"Exactly," Riley replied. "No birds, no bugs, nothing."

"Come to think of it," I began. "I haven't heard any wildlife in a while. The mosquitos haven't been bothering me much either."

"That's right," Riley said. "There's a hurricane coming."

~ 13 ~

The early morning approached with the first bands of the hurricane moving inland. I headed just before the tree line, pulled out my binoculars, and checked the ranch. I could just make out the crude house where the outlaws were staying in the faint light. I didn't see any movement. Then I headed back to our camp.

"Alright," I said. "This is it. Do you all remember the plan?"

"I'm ready," replied Aiden.

Riley didn't say anything. He shook his head once in agreement, very confidently.

I put my belt on and placed both holsters on the left side so I could easily grab the guns with my right hand. The straps around my shoulders made carrying the weight of the guns much easier. Then I grabbed Luis' rifle.

"Remember," I said, "I will fire the first shot. Then we all move in if we can."

We all separated and went our ways. I circled around but kept low, using the thick, wet woods as cover. Once I got in a position where I could see the front door and one side of the house, I moved in closer. I lay low and crawled out from the protection of the woods. I still wanted to use my left hand to hold the rifle like normal, but it was impossible. I looked around while I lay on my stomach. I found an old twig that forked out in two separate directions.

This will work, I thought to myself. I started breaking the twig until it was shaped like a rough-looking "Y." I planted the bottom of the "Y" in the ground and placed the barrel of Luis' rifle in the fork.

Perfect, now I can hold the gun still, I thought.

I looked for the others. Riley had taken a position behind the house just in the woods. If Alaster and his men managed to get past our gunfire, they would use the cover of the woods to run and hide. Riley was perfect for the job. He knew the Glades like the back of his hand. He would surprise anyone who tried to escape in that direction.

Aiden was positioned behind the stable. He was waiting for the first shot. On the signal, he was to move toward the stables and use the building as cover while he guarded the opposite side of the cabin and part of the front.

This time, we were going to be the ones surprising everyone. I could feel it.

Hours passed. I looked at my watch. It was 12 noon before I heard any signs of life. Someone in the cabin was moving around. Then someone started talking.

My volunteers and I were quiet. I put my head lower and cocked the rifle. I pointed the weapon right at the front door. A few minutes went by before it opened. Then a figure appeared out of the darkness. It was the man who climbed into the way car to help Alaster weeks earlier. He stepped out on the porch, stopped, and stretched his arms. His old torn undershirt and pants were on clear display. His suspenders were swinging at his sides.

I fired my rifle. The outlaw stumbled backward through the door. I looked through my binoculars. His feet disappeared into the darkness of the cabin as someone dragged him in and shut the door.

Then the window shutters on the cabin swung open with a couple of rifles pointed in my direction. Gunshots echoed from the trees, and bullets buzzed all around me. I was not sure they could see me, but I began firing back. I emptied the Colt rifle into the window before the shutters slammed tight.

A minute went by when the shutter on the opposite window opened. Aiden began pouring bullets into it. I heard someone yell, followed by a loud thud on the floor. The noise of the shutter slamming closed followed.

Another minute went by, and I saw the front door crack open. Someone was trying to get a better view. I grabbed one of my Colt dragoons and aimed at the door. I emptied the revolver into the door before it slammed shut.

As I grabbed my other revolver, I saw a man take off running from behind the cabin. He was wearing some long johns with a pair of boots. He must have escaped from the window. I managed to get a couple of shots off before he disappeared into the woods. A couple of minutes went by when I heard a loud yell come from that direction. No doubt it was Riley at work. I can only imagine what happened, but I knew he got the man.

All got silent. There was one man left, Alaster. The front door opened again. Aiden started firing at it. Alaster returned fire. I heard another yell, but this time, it came from the stable. It was Aiden.

That was the catalyst that my temper needed. I felt it just like the old days. I lost all sense of everything around me. It traveled up my neck, passed my ears, and then I was consumed in anger. I stood up from my spot in clear view of the cabin. The front door swung open, and Alaster ran out. He stopped and began firing at me until he emptied the gun. The bullets buzzed all around me. I began walking toward him, and he stumbled backward. I began firing my gun: one shot, and it just missed Alaster; another shot, and he jumped out of the way; a third shot, and it hit him in the chest, and he fell onto his back with a thud when he hit the saturated ground. I walked right up to him and looked directly down at his face. I cocked the gun one last time to finish him off, but it clicked. I was out of bullets. Alaster looked up at me. I put the revolver back in its holster and pulled out the pepperbox that Alaster had laughed at on the train. I pointed it at his face.

"I was wondering when you were going to show up," said Alaster. "I knew you weren't too far behind me."

I didn't say anything. I just looked at him.

Alaster smiled and tried to talk down the situation like we were honorable adversaries or something. "That's why I paid Luis $30. I thought if I waited at that trading post, we could ambush you. It wasn't hard to get Luis to give you away. He hates us Americans. He misses old Spanish Florida. One of my guys accidentally hit him when they were aiming at you."

The bands from the cyclone were getting worse as the storm moved further inland.

"Do you have any idea what it's like to live here?" continued Alaster. He changed his tone. He was now more direct. "You have to fight for everything. It's a conquest every day. Yes, I took this land and these cattle, even these horses. Others did the same."

I didn't say anything.

"Then there were the wars," Alaster continued. "The Seminoles never let up. They would come and destroy everything.

The only way you can settle your differences here is with a gun. If you don't kill them, they will kill you.

I didn't say anything.

"Do you have any idea what it's like to starve?" Alaster asked. "I do. I raised myself. And one day, I vowed to never starve again, no matter the costs. The outlaws here taught me how to keep my stomach full."

I didn't say anything.

"Death was a natural occurrence. If the Seminoles and outlaws didn't get you, the environment did. My parents were homesteaders. They died of a fever and left us kids to fend for ourselves."

I still didn't say anything.

"Don't you understand?" Alaster asked. He looked as if he wanted mercy.

"I do," I replied. "The four horsemen have reached the end of their ride."

"Call it what you want," Alaster said. "I survived."

I cocked the pepperbox and moved it closer to Alaster's face. His eyes became the size of saucers, but he refused to surrender.

Riley appeared from the direction of the stable.

"Ethan," Riley began. "Aiden is alright. He got hit in the shoulder, but he will be fine. We need to get him to a doctor."

I didn't say anything. I thought about young Aiden with his life ahead of him. I thought about the sheriff of St. Marks. I thought about the trouble along the railroads and our horses that he killed. I thought about Luis betraying me and all the other people Alaster put in harm's way.

My temper had reached its breaking point. I moved the gun closer to Alaster's face and stood directly above him. I looked right into his scared eyes.

"Ethan," Riley said. "Don't forget about your wife and children."

The words resonated. I looked at the gun in my right hand. I thought about my wife in front of the staircase and the conversation we had. I felt like I was in the middle of an exam.

I fought the urge. My hand was itching to pull the trigger, but I lowered the gun and un-cocked it. I slowly placed it in my pocket. Then I bent over, grabbed the empty revolver from Alaster's hand, and looked at it. He laid his head on the wet ground and gave a sigh of relief. When Alaster least expected it, I turned the revolver around in my hand and hit him in the face with the butt of his gun.

Alaster grabbed his face and began to rock back and forth in the mud. "Damn you!"

"Faith would be proud," Riley said with a smile.

"If only she were here to witness it," I replied.

The rain stopped briefly, but the breeze from the storm continued to pick up.

"You never know," Riley replied.

~ 14 ~

The next few days went by quickly. We had arrived in Pine Level not long after the shootout. A local rancher, glad that we had put a stop to Alaster's rustling activities, invited us to stay at his ranch while the hurricane passed and Aiden and Alaster recovered from their wounds. When Aiden was ready, we joined the rancher and his cowboys as they drove a herd of cattle to a market in Tampa. When we arrived, the rancher booked passage to St. Marks on a sidewheel steamer for Aiden, Riley, and Alaster, and me.

By this point, we were docking in St. Marks. We entered the city like the forgotten four of the Narváez expedition when they entered Mexico City so many centuries ago. The incident with Alaster was old news, and everyone in the small town had moved on to other things.

Despite clear skies, the new moon made for a dark night as we found ourselves loading up on the same way car Alaster had escaped from well over a month ago. The trains were now using lanterns so they could work through the night to keep up with the cotton shipments. The railway workers were on top of their game, too. By the time it was ready for us to board, our horses had already been transferred from the ship to a flat car at the end of the train. They wasted no time.

Riley and Aiden climbed up into the car. They both reached down and picked up Alaster by the shoulders. Alaster's hands were both tied with a rope around his waist, so he couldn't do much to help. We refused to take any chances this time around. As they picked him up, I began to help by pulling up on the rope with my right hand. I still was not accustomed to using my left hand in its new state. While I struggled, another person came by and grabbed the rope on the opposite side of Alaster. It was the conductor from before.

He put his damaged hand up in front of his face and wiggled his remaining fingers. "You get used to it after a while. It just takes time."

While Aiden kept a gun on Alaster, Riley and the conductor helped me up into the way car. Once I was in the car, the conductor headed toward the front of the train. Aiden, Alaster, and I resumed our positions as before. We sat down on the floor with our backs against the wall, with Riley joining us this time.

Two short whistles blew from the locomotive, and the way car began to jerk as the train's couplers stretched. After a couple of minutes, the train was rolling down the track. The doors were wide open. As the way car bounced along, two lanterns hanging from the ceiling burned brightly and swung with the motion of the car. The wood burning stove still had some hot coals in it.

I looked out the door toward the dark woods, more alert than before in the event that Alaster had another trick up his sleeve. I briefly saw the dim light of the lantern shine on the remains of the destroyed flat car as it rolled by the door. We were back where we started. Poetic in a way, I looked at Alaster. He looked down at the floor like a defeated man. He knew what awaited him in Tallahassee. His days were numbered.

A few minutes went by when a railroad worker climbed in from the roof. He slid the doors shut.

"Let's see if we can warm it up some in here."

The railroad worker began putting some wood in the stove. He looked at me. "Are you the major?"

"That's right," I said.

"The conductor told me to tell you that we will be in Tallahassee quick. We have no scheduled stops."

~ 15 ~

One short whistle blew from the locomotive as it slowed to enter the station. The train couplers clanged as the cars rolled into one another. The engineer started swinging the bell of the locomotive back and forth as it came to a stop. The railroad worker in the way car swung open the door as we all rose from the floor.

The platform was dimly lit with lanterns in the early morning hours. When we exited the way car, our horses were already being unloaded from the flat car. We stepped down from the platform and put Alaster on top of one of the spare horses. Then we mounted our horses. Aiden and I got along each side of Alaster with our rifles pointed at him. We let our horses walk at a slow pace as we kept an eye on the buildings and alleyways in case Alaster had any other men ready to rescue him. Riley brought up the rear.

When we arrived at the sheriff's office, Aiden and I dismounted and pulled Alaster down from his horse.

"Riley," I began, "keep an eye out just in case. We're almost finished with him."

I lowered my rifle, opened the door to the sheriff's office, and led Alaster and Aiden into the building. Aiden kept a rifle on Alaster the whole while.

A man with a thick mustache and sideburns was at the desk drinking a cup of coffee. He stood up. "It can't be! Are you Major Tucker? Is this the man that caused that trouble along the Tallahassee Railroad?"

"That's right," I said.

"Hell," he replied. "We'd given up on you all. After a month had passed, we didn't think you were coming back."

"I always see my jobs to the end," I responded.

"No doubt for sure," he replied. He looked at Alaster as he pulled his keys from his desk. "Mr. Alaster, we have a cell in the back that we have been holding in reserve for you."

The sheriff led us to the cell and opened the door. Aiden and I untied the ropes and placed Alaster in the cell. Then the sheriff slammed the door shut, and Aiden and I lowered our weapons. Alaster again did not say anything. He sat down on the cot and stared at the floor. Now, I was certain. I could tell from the way he was acting. No one was coming. Alaster was truly a defeated man.

"Would you boys like some breakfast?" asked the sheriff.

Aiden looked at me. I looked at the sheriff. "No, thank you," I replied. "We have one more stop to make."

With that, Aiden and I left the office and mounted our horses. All three of us began making our way to the adjutant general's office.

I looked over at Aiden. "How's the wound? Does it still hurt?"

"It's getting better," he said. "It hurts some."

"You ready for that civil war?" I asked.

"I don't know," he replied. "I was excited before, but I forgot about the other people shooting back at you."

I smiled and said, "No doubt about that."

When we arrived at Ryder's office, I dismounted from my horse and tied it to the hitching post.

I looked at Aiden and Riley. They were still on their horses. "You two wait here. This shouldn't take long."

I walked into the office, and the secretary recognized me from before.

"Hello, sir," replied the secretary. "I will tell the adjutant general that you are here." He stood up and disappeared in the back. I looked out the window. Aiden and Riley were talking to a woman on the boardwalk. I could see the blonde hair on the back of her head. She was wearing a green dress and jacket. Then my two sons ran up to her and stopped beside her. It was Faith!

I heard footsteps coming from the hallway. I looked back and saw Ryder trailing behind the secretary. The secretary sat down at his desk and went back to work. Ryder reached out and shook my hand.

"The job's done," I said. "Alaster is at the sheriff's office."

"Job well done," Ryder was much more relaxed than before. "I'm going to be honest. I wasn't sure if you were going to make it back. Your last letter said he robbed a train around Starke, then I didn't hear back."

I held up my hand and showed it to him. "Alaster fought us like a cornered rattlesnake as we closed in on him."

"It looks like it," Ryder replied. He did not show any sympathy. "What's important is you're back safe, and Alaster is behind bars. The governor will be happy." He reached into his pocket, pulled out two envelopes, and handed them to me. "Here's your pay."

I slipped the envelopes in my pocket and looked back at Ryder.

"One of my men got hurt as well," I replied. I don't know why I continued to bring it up. I knew Ryder wouldn't care. I guess I wanted to see if he would show any sign of caring at all.

"Is that a fact?" said Ryder. "Alaster really was a tough customer."

"Yes, he was." I pointed out the window toward Aiden. "Aiden was shot in the shoulder."

"It's a good thing he's young," Ryder replied. "He'll pull through."

I could tell by his tone Ryder didn't care. Then I pointed at Riley. "And Riley there," I began. "We would have never tracked Alaster down without him. He helped us through the terrain, and he fought Alaster's men."

"Good, good," Ryder replied. "We could always use good men like him."

"Good," I replied back. "I'm glad you brought that up. You think you could use him in the militia? He's hoping to play a big role in it in the years ahead."

Ryder took another look at Riley through the window. Then he looked at me. He was hesitant to respond.

"He's part Creek," I said. "He helped us track down the Seminoles during the wars. He hates them all."

Ryder seemed a bit relieved with that remark. "I will certainly consider it," he replied. Ryder then turned and walked back down the hall to his office. He was trying to brush me off.

Just before Ryder began to open the door, I stopped him. "Ryder, I'm done. The militia is just not what it was under your leadership. I tender my resignation."

His secretary looked up at me.

"You can't..." Ryder began.

I pulled my Colt dragoon out from its holster and waved it a couple of times at him like I was contemplating what to do. The secretary's eyes were as wide as platters. Ryder was scared to death. I could see his knuckles turn white as his hand grasped the doorknob tighter. Then I looked out the window and saw my wife and kids. I paused for a minute then put the gun back in its holster.

"I'm done, Ryder. You don't know upright people when they're right in front of your eyes."

Ryder quickly opened the door, entered the room, and shut the door behind him. I turned and walked out of the office.

I walked to the very edge of the boardwalk toward Aiden and Riley. I paused for a minute, thinking of the right words to say. "The adjutant general thanks you both for your service. He says you are both great assets to the state. We are officially dismissed."

Aiden spoke first. "Thank you, sir." He paused for a moment. "It's been educational."

"You just take care of your wounds," I replied.

Aiden saluted me and shook Riley's hand. I reached into my pocket and handed him his envelope. As he rode off, he tipped his old hat to my wife. Riley and I just laughed.

"Maybe one day he'll get rid of that thing," I told Riley.

"Hopefully," said Riley. "Did the adjutant general say anything about me joining the militia?"

I thought about it for a minute. "The adjutant general said he would certainly consider it." Riley smiled at the response. I didn't want to give him all the details of the conversation and have him give up his hopes. Besides, if a war did occur between the states, it would probably escalate quickly, in which case, they would take anyone who is breathing.

"Riley," I reached out to shake his hand, "you take care of yourself and your family. Thank you for everything."

"Good luck with your wife," he said. "I'm sure things will work out."

Riley turned his horse away from the boardwalk and began his long ride back home.

I turned and looked at Faith standing on the boardwalk in the pre-dawn light of the morning—pretty as always. Our children were watching. I removed my hat with my right hand and walked up to her. She looked at my left hand.

"Oh my God, Ethan!"

She grabbed my hand and began to examine it. She saw the bullet hole in my jacket. Her hands began to shake as she examined the damage.

"I came as soon as I heard you arrived at the station," Faith began. "I thought I would find you here at Ryder's office."

"I'm sorry, honey. I meant to write more. It just didn't work out."

"I was worried sick after your last letter. You were near Starke. I thought the worst may have happened when I didn't receive anything else."

"It would have had it not been for a local doctor."

Faith grabbed my other hand and looked up at me. "Riley told me about your trip. He told me everything." Faith put her arms around me, and I put my arms around her.

"Ethan," Faith said, "please come back home."

Then both our boys came up and put their arms around us. "Please come back home, dad."

As I untied my horse and mounted it, my wife and children climbed into a buggy pulled by a single horse. The early morning sun shined down on us as we began our journey back home. The sun began to warm me up.

I looked at Faith as my horse walked alongside their buggy. "I feel like I've been reborn."